Grandma's Silent Auction
March
BY: Michael James

Copyright © 2020 by Michael James

All rights reserved.

No part of this book may be reproduced in any form or by any electronic or mechanical means, including information storage and retrieval systems, without written permission from the author, except for the use of brief quotations in a book review.

CHAPTER ONE
CIARA

I entered the restroom at the airport and set Alaska on the counter in her little carrier. I look at myself in the mirror. God, I look horrible. I didn't bother applying makeup this morning, I knew it would just get ruined if I did. Saying goodbye to Malcolm wasn't easy. It wasn't easy to say goodbye to Hawk, either. I thought it would be easier being this is the second time I've had to do this, but I was wrong. So very wrong! How is it possible to have feelings for two men? Malcolm and Hawk are not very much alike. Malcolm is my sweet, caring, loving sexy nerd. Hawk is my wild, fun-loving, sexy race car driver. Malcolm brings the romance level and Hawk brings the live on the edge of your seat level. I am anxious to see what Warrick will bring to the table.

Warrick Winthrop, I know nothing about him because I still don't have the three-ring binder my Grams supplied me with. It's somewhere in my apartment. Being back in the city not far from my apartment, maybe I can find time to scoot home and retrieve it. I only knew this because I had to call Grams to ask. I think she was irritated with me for not being prepared. She really didn't like it that I didn't come home when I was supposed to. I spent the extra days with Hawk instead. If I hadn't broken her rules, I would have had the information I needed. She also wouldn't have had to make new arrangements for me to meet someone by the name of Barbara Melton at the airport. I know nothing about her except for her name. I was supposed to get off the plane and search for her holding a sign with my name on it. Oops, I broke another rule by not doing that because here I am in the airport bathroom trying to compose myself.

I look at my puppy in her carrier. She seems content since she's chewing on her chew toy filled with peanut butter. I guess the flight didn't bother her at all. I look back at my reflection in the mirror. I touch underneath my eyes that are a bit puffy. Christ, I've cried more in the last two months than I have in the last couple of years.

I open my purse and get out some makeup and

start applying some foundation. I am not going to go into my full routine, but I should at least make myself look presentable. Okay, maybe I'm just stalling a little bit, too. I am not really jumping for joy that I will soon be meeting the third guy from Grams secretive silent auction. I can't fully say that there's not a smidgen of curiosity in me to see what Warrick is all about. I just don't want to get any feelings for him. I already have feelings for two men, I do not need to add a third guy into the mix.

I put all my makeup back in my purse. I then run my fingers through my hair. I glance at Alaska. *"Okay, girl, I guess we better go find this Barbara lady before someone puts out a missing person report on us."* I pick the carrier up and put the strap over my shoulder. *"Here goes nothing, Alaska."*

I exit the restroom not knowing for sure where I should go. I am looking up at the signs that hang down from the ceiling. I should probably find my luggage first. I am not sure where to go for that since I arrived on Hawk's private plane.

"Ciara Verbank, right?"

"Umm, that's me."

"I'm Barbara Melton." She holds out her hand. I reach out mine and shake her hand. *"I saw you exit*

the terminal and go right for the restroom. I took the liberty of getting your luggage."

"Oh!"

"If you are ready the car is waiting."

"I'm ready."

I walk beside Barbara who is wheeling my luggage. I tried to take it from her, but she said she had it. When we get outside a Towne car is waiting. The driver takes my suitcase and puts it in the trunk. I get in the backseat and Barbara gets in on the other side. I feel awkward. I don't know if I should strike up a conversation or not. Denise, Malcolm's assistant was friendly and so was Malcolm's driver, Pat. But after meeting Bethany, I feel a little bit cautious. Maybe I should reserve myself and not keep getting friendly with so many people.

"So, Mr. Winthrop is still tied up and won't be free until after five. It's almost three, so we are going to go right to his house and wait for Shay."

"Okay. Who is Shay?"

"His daughter."

"Oh, I wasn't aware Warrick is a father."

"You will love Shay. She's brilliant and so damn cute."

"How old is she?"

"She'll be six next month."

I am a tad bit thrown back by this. I know nothing about kids. I have no idea how to be a mother figure. Do I even need to be a mother figure? I'm sure the little girl has a mother. Maybe I'll just be like a friend to her. I don't know how to be friends with an almost six-year-old. I am freaking out a little on the inside. I am going to mess this all up. I just know I will. God, help me!

"What do you do for Warrick? Or are you family?"

"I'm the nanny."

"Are you a live-in nanny?"

"I go home to my husband every night unless Warrick is traveling."

"How long have you been a nanny?"

"Since Shay was born, but I became a nanny when I was eighteen. I quit for a while to be home for my own son."

"How old is he?"

"He's in his twenties. He recently joined the military."

Barbara seems nice enough. I wonder if she'll talk about Warrick if I ask her questions. I am sure she was told to keep her lips sealed. However, the suspense is killing me.

"So, he has a daughter, what else should I know about him?"

"Oh, we are here!"

Well, there went that question right out the window. I look out the window. Wow! His home is very nice and very big. It is a light-colored brick home with a gated driveway. There is a two-car garage and it seems his property is a decent size. The car pulls right up out front instead of at the garage. His driveway is a horseshoe shape. Which is why the driver can stop out front.

Barbara doesn't wait for the driver to open her door, so I don't either. I put the strap of Alaska's carrier over my shoulder. I'm sure she's going to need to go potty soon. It's been hours since she's been out of her little tote.

The driver gets my luggage from the trunk and Barbara is right there to take it. I follow her up the paved steps to the front door. She enters a code on the keyboard and enters.

"I'll give you a tour then I'll show you your room."

"Okay. Oh and I should probably let my puppy out to go potty."

"I'm not sure Mr. Winthrop will like that you have

a puppy. So after you take her out maybe it's best you put her back in the carrier."

Well, I sure am not leaving her crated for the next month! Even if I break the rules and live in my own apartment the entire month. I refuse to have Alaska penned up and I sure as hell will not be separated from her. We are a package deal.

CHAPTER TWO
CIARA

I have been outside for the past forty-five minutes with Alaska. I have been thinking about Barbara's comment that Warrick might not allow my puppy to be here. I am all for respecting his wishes, I hope he'll respect mine if I choose not to stay here. I am hoping she was just being cautious because of her uncertainty about the situation. I also have to take into consideration that possibly he or his daughter could have an allergy to animal dandruff, fur or whatever it is that causes people to have an allergic reaction to animals. I would completely understand if that were the case. I am trying to remain calm until I know the facts.

"Are you alright? You have been out here a while."

"I'm fine. Alaska has been in her carrier for quite awhile, so I want to give her some play time."

"I know what I said came out wrong. I am unsure how Warrick feels about having animals in his home. I just want you to wait until he's here to make his own decisions."

"Are one of them allergic to animals?" Barbara has a seat next to me on the patio. *"Either way, I do understand your concern."*

"Not that I'm aware of. You don't know Warrick. It's just that he's very protective of Shay."

"You are right I don't know him or his daughter. I see nothing wrong with being protective of the people you love. That is why I decided to stay out here for a while."

Barbara looks at her watch. *"I have to go and get Shay off the bus."*

"Should I just stay out here until he gets home to introduce me to his daughter?"

"Not at all. Warrick told her a friend was coming to visit."

A friend. I watch over my shoulder as Barbara goes back into the house. I'm not sure I am ready for this. It's stressful enough having to meet a new guy and to add a kid into the mix has my nerves on edge even more. I wish I were meeting Warrick first. I don't know what he told his daughter about me.

I glance around the yard. I honestly want to run and hide. I should have told Barbara I'd be more comfortable waiting until Warrick was here. As I said before, I know nothing about kids. I never even so much as babysat before.

"Pray I don't mess this up, Alaska. I may need all the prayers I can get."

I glance over my shoulder once again when I hear the back door open. I smile when the little girl's eyes light up. She comes running toward me.

"You have a puppy? Can I play with it?"

"Sure." I set Alaska to the ground and Shay tried to snap her fingers. My puppy goes right over to her. *"Her name is Alaska."*

"She's so cute!"

"Thank you."

The two of them play for a short time. I sit here and watch. Shay is a very cute little girl with her brown pigtails, big brown eyes, and she has the cutest laugh. I can't help but wonder if she looks like her daddy or mommy.

"Shay, your after school snack is ready."

Shay looks right at me. *"Can I bring Alaska inside with me?"*

"You can but she will have to go in her carrier."

"Why?"

"I don't have permission from your daddy yet to have her here."

"Can we come back outside after my snack?"

"Sure, if it's okay with Barbara."

Shay stands, picks Alaska up, and hands her over to me. I put Alaska in her carrier. My puppy barks and Shay laughs. Goddamn, she is a cutie. She takes my hand.

"If we eat fast we can come right back out."

I smile and hide my laugh. Personally, I like the way she thinks. Since I don't know the layout of the house because I never got the tour Barbara talked about, I follow Shay to the kitchen. Barbara has Shay's snack waiting for her at the breakfast bar. I put Alaska on the floor and Shay pats the seat for me to sit next to her. I look at Barbara as Shay picks up her chocolate chip cookie.

"Where is Ciara's cookie and milk?"

"Oh, I'm fine."

"You don't want a cookie?" She asks me.

"There are plenty to spare," Barbara states.

"Okay, sure I'll have a cookie."

Shay bites into her cookie again. *"Barb makes the best ones."*

When she gives me a cookie and bite into it, I have to agree it is very good. Shay eats her cookie as fast as she can and drinks down her milk. She gets down from the breakfast bar.

"I have to go and wash my hands then I will be ready to go back outside."

She runs off and I giggle. Barbara cleans up after Shay. *"She's so cute."*

"I know. She is a very lovable child. I worry how this month will impact her."

"Because of me?"

"Yes. I worry she will become attached to you and then you'll be gone."

"I have no intentions of hurting her."

"I know you don't, but I still worry."

"Understandable."

I like Barbara. I can see that she really cares about Shay's wellbeing. I also think that Barbara is going to be keeping her eyes on me. I can't blame her. I am the outsider here and she's been in Shay's life since she was born. I would be the same way if I were in her shoes.

"Okay, my hands are all washed. I'm ready."

"What are you ready for?" A man's voice says from behind us.

"Daddy!" She goes running to her dad.

Here goes nothing. I turn around in my seat as Warrick enters the kitchen. Oh my, he is a very tall, well-built man. He picks Shay up and hugs her to his body. She looks super tiny compared to his big frame. Shay grabs his face and gives her daddy a kiss.

"How is my best girl today?"

"I'm good. Ciara and I are going outside so that I can play with Alaska again."

He looks right at me and smiles. *"Who is Alaska?"*

"Her puppy."

"I told Ciara I was unsure if you would want a puppy running freely in the house."

"Ciara is our guest. That means so is her puppy."

I smile. That is such a huge relief. Shay grabs her dad's face again. *"So I can let her out?"*

"Yes, as long as it is okay with Ciara."

He puts Shay to her feet. *"Can I, can I?"*

"Of course you can."

Warrick comes over to where I am. Damn he looks even taller standing so close to me. *"Hi."*

I repeat his words. *"Hi."*

"Have you settled in yet?"

"I haven't."

"I figured since your luggage is in the foyer. How about I give you the grand tour."

"Umm, sure." I glance at my puppy. I am a little worried about leaving her unattended.

"Shay, can you watch Alaska while Daddy shows Ciara the house?"

"You bet I will."

Warrick tells Barbara she is done for the day and that she won't be needed tomorrow. He adds that she might not be needed the rest of the week. She frowns, unhappy with hearing that news, possibly? I wonder if it's because she can't keep an eye on me or if she didn't want the time off.

"Looks like I'll be hitting up the movie theater tomorrow. Ciara, it's been a pleasure to meet you."

"Same to you, Barbara."

Barbara gathers her purse and keys from the counter and then leaves the kitchen after giving Shay a huge goodbye. I peek through my lashes at Warrick. My stomach knots up and my palms become sweaty. I am about to spend alone time with a man I don't even know.

CHAPTER THREE
WARRICK

My practice ran over today. I was disappointed that I couldn't pick Ciara up myself from the airport. It would have been nice to meet the girl before my daughter did. It is what it is, though. Life can't stop just because I decided to give love a second shot. I still have a job to do and right now it is important as it's getting whipped back into shape. Our season is nearing. Spring training starts next week. I picked a hell of a time to disrupt mine and Shay's routine. Although, I am hopeful Ciara isn't a disruption. I am hopeful that love can conquer all. I sure do miss the companionship of a woman being in my life.

Once I was done with batting practice, there was a team meeting with the management team. I know this meeting is important, however, I couldn't help but daydream of the girl I am about to meet. Ciara's grandmother, Millie reached out to me, my first thought was this lady is crazy. Then I saw Ciara's picture and I couldn't pass up the chance to meet her, date her and possibly fall in love. The girl made my heart skip a few beats if you know what I mean. If it doesn't work out at least the money goes to a good cause. I will also know if I am ready to enter the dating world again. Honestly, I am not a hundred percent sure I am.

I entered the house and I heard the voices in the kitchen. I figured that was right where they would be since Barbara keeps a tight schedule. I know it's snack time. The woman is amazing with my daughter. I would kinda be a little lost if it weren't for her guidance and advice. When I hired her, I hired more than a nanny, I got the whole package. Barbara loves Shay as if she were her own child. I never have to worry about my daughter's wellbeing with her watching over Shay.

"What are you ready for?" I asked as I entered the kitchen.

"Daddy!" Shay comes running into my arms as she does every day. This is one of the best times of the day. I cherish each hug of excitement from her. I

know this won't last forever. *"How is my best girl today?"*

"I'm good. Ciara and I are going outside so that I can play with Alaska again."

"Who is Alaska?"

"Her puppy."

Barbara says, *"I told Ciara I was unsure if you would want a puppy running freely in the house."*

"Ciara is our guest. That means so is her puppy." I can see the relief wash over Ciara's body.

"So I can let her out?"

"Yes, as long as it is okay with Ciara."

I put Shay to her feet. *"Can I, can I?"* she asks Ciara

"Of course you can."

I walk over to where she sits at the breakfast bar. *"Hi."* well that was lamer than I was going for.

She repeats my words. *"Hi."*

"Have you settled in yet?"

"I haven't."

"I figured since your luggage is in the foyer. How about I give you the grand tour."

"I would like that."

"Shay, can you be a big girl and watch the puppy for us?"

Before I start to give Ciara the tour of the house, I

tell Barbara I don't need her tomorrow. She seems disappointed. She knows her time with Shay will be less and less for the next few months. I have spring training starting and that means traveling. Barbara doesn't travel with us unless I absolutely need her to.

I show Ciara the downstairs part of the house first. The living room, family room, dining room, playroom, home office, downstairs bathroom, and the sunroom. She already saw the kitchen and the back patio. Sometimes I think this house is too big for just me and Shay.

"Ready to see the upstairs?"

"I am."

I grab her luggage in the foyer. *"I thought I was supposed to take you shopping?"*

"That is my Grams rules. I find it crazy as I have my own clothing line."

I joke. *"You best not get me into trouble with Millie, she is a feisty one."*

She laughs. *"Yes, she is, but I got your back."*

We stop outside the first door. *"This is my shoe room. Athletes can't have enough sneakers to wear."*

"Oh." I open the door and allow her in first. I was just joking about this being my shoe room. She slaps my arm. *"You got me. I thought you were serious."*

I laugh. *"This is your room."* I set her suitcase

down near the closet. I figure it will be a good time to tell her we will be traveling next week. *"My spring training starts next week."*

"Oh, you play baseball?"

"Yep, it was my first true love."

"Are you in the big league?"

"Yes, I am. I wear the pinstripes."

"How cool is that! I've never been to a game before. I've always wanted to go. Every year I say I'm going but then something comes up."

"Good, I look forward to taking you to your first game. Ready to see more?"

"I sure am."

We go across the hall to my room. Then to Shay's room. I don't bother showing her the other spare rooms.

"I was thinking we could go out to dinner. Would you like that?"

"Would you be upset if we stayed in and maybe ordered take-out?"

"Sounds fine with me. I'll take you out tomorrow night."

When Ciara smiles, it lights up the room. This woman is so damn beautiful. How is a girl like her single? Someone should have swept her off her feet by now. That makes me wonder if one of the other guys have done that. Have they beaten me to the plate? I cross my fingers that they haven't. I am just about ready to ask her a question, but she beats me to it.

"Why did you do this? I mean, why me? Never mind you don't need to answer that."

"I will answer." I rub the back of my neck and hope I don't fuck this up. *"I saw your profile and I couldn't resist getting to know you."*

"Can I ask you another question? You don't have to answer if you don't want to."

"You can. How else are we going to get to know each other if we don't ask each other things, right?"

"Shay's mother, is she in the picture?"

I didn't expect that question. *"No. I have full custody of her."* I don't know why I didn't tell her the full truth. I guess I am just not ready to give her that part of me.

"So, I don't need to worry about a jealous ex or anything? You seem nice and Shay is lovely, I just don't want to be in the middle of any drama."

"You have nothing to worry about."

We went back downstairs and I found the take-out menus, we decided on Mexican. I probably ordered way too much food for the three of us. Shay and Ciara are playing with the puppy. I didn't know anything about the dog. Shay seems to really like it. After this month is over with, I have a feeling my daughter will be begging me for one. I suppose it would be better than a cat. I really don't have the time for an animal regardless if it were a dog, cat or horse. My lifestyle isn't the best for an animal. We travel so much by plane and bus. I guess this month will be a test.

CHAPTER FOUR
CIARA

I voluntarily said I'd clean up dinner while Warrick gets Shay ready for bed. We had Mexican take-out and ate in the living room. Warrick and Shay call that carpet picnics. I was blessed enough to be part of it. They told me it's their thing and I am the only person who has been welcomed to join their private picnic. I have to admit, I really enjoyed it. It made me feel special. I found it more enjoyable than going to some fancy restaurant. Not only was the food great, but so was watching Shay's favorite movie while we ate. It's been a very long time since I've watched a Disney movie. I forgot what it is like to sink back into being a kid again, watching fairy tales unfold. I have to say, meeting these two has been very delightful.

I put all the leftovers in the refrigerator. Warrick

ordered enough food to feed two families. I am full from taste testing everything he had ordered. It was worth every bite. When I am finished in the kitchen I sneak upstairs. I bypass my room and stand outside of Shay's room. I overhear him reading her a goodnight story. I lean on the wall just outside the door and listen. I feel as if I'm intruding. It's rude to be eavesdropping on them. As much as I don't want to overstep their privacy, I don't find myself able to walk away. I stay in my place until I hear him say, the end. He tells her goodnight and that he loves her. She does the same. I push off the wall, ready to walk away when I hear her tell him she likes me. It warms my heart. I like her, too. I pop my head into the room.

"Goodnight, Shay."

"Night, Ciara. I'm really glad you are here."

"Me, too."

Warrick comes to the door and shuts the lights off. *"Sweet dreams, Nugget."* Nugget! That's cute. He shuts the door. *"Care to have a nightcap with me?"*

"I'd like that."

Warrick tells me he'll get us a glass of wine and that I should go ahead and make myself comfortable in the living room. I do just that. I turn the television off before I get comfortable. I must say, the man's couch is very cozy. It's the type that you sink right into. I lean on the armrest and kick my feet up.

"Your wine, madame."

I giggle at his lightheartedness. *"Thank you so much, kind sir."*

Warrick sits at the opposite end of the couch. *"Shay isn't the only one that's glad you're here. I am as well."*

I smile. *"I was eavesdropping. Do you read to her every night?"*

"I try. It's harder when we travel."

"Shay always travels with you?"

"Not always. I try to balance her life as much as possible. I want her to attend school and I want her with me."

"It must be difficult when you two aren't together."

"It is, but we manage quite well. She understands I have a job to do and that she does as well. It's not always easy being an only parent. I wouldn't trade her for anything, though."

I really want to ask about Shay's mother. Again, I decided against it. I'm sure he'll open up about that when he's comfortable with me. Until then, I'll just enjoy getting to know them. After all, it's him I'm here for. I am not here to pry into his past.

Warrick talks about tomorrow as we sit here having a glass of wine. He's telling me that he has to go to the stadium for a few hours and would like for me to join him. Shay has school, but we'll be done before she gets out. He has to be there by nine. I am thrilled about going since I haven't ever been to the ball field before. I am a bit nervous about the possibility of meeting his teammates. After the bullshit I went through with Bethany, Hawk's assistant, I will be more cautious about meeting new people. I don't need to add to the stress I'm already been through.

I tell Warrick that my shop isn't too far from here. I tell him my best friend Porter works for me. I was hesitant to ask if he'd like to see it. I caved and asked because honestly, I miss work. I miss my friend. We haven't really talked all that much. I was excited that he said he'd love to see it. We are planning on going once Shay gets home. He added we can go out to dinner afterwards. It makes me happy that he seems delighted that I asked him to see inside my world.

I yawn. It's been quite a long day. Once again, it's also been a rollercoaster of emotions. Leaving Hawk and then getting swept into a new man's home on the same day was probably not a bright idea on my part. I have to admit, I was caught up in the moment of wanting to be with Hawk a few more days. I probably should have gone home for those few days to adjust to the change. I am learning this as I go. I don't think there's a book of rules on how to date ten men in ten months. Well, I guess there is if I were to follow Grams rules. I pretty much have gone against her rules.

"If you are tired, I don't want to keep you up. We have almost a full month to get to know each other."

"What made you do this?"

"I have my reasons. It is not a short story. We have plenty of time to discuss this further. I'm curious as to why you have done this as well."

"That is a short story."

"How about we call it a night. I for one need my beauty sleep," he jokes. No you don't, I want to scream. *"I'll clean up. You go ahead and go to bed."*

I get up from the cozy couch. *"Thanks for letting me join your carpet picnic. It made me feel special."*

"You are welcome! I'm sure Shay will try to have more of those while you are with us."

"Goodnight, Warrick."

"Goodnight, Ciara."

I make my way to my new room. I remember doing this two months ago when I met Malcolm. I didn't last very long, me sleeping in the room he gave me. I need to make a real effort this time with staying put. I'm sure Warrick doesn't want me sneaking into his room with his daughter right down the hall. I sure as hell don't want to be the one to confuse an almost six year old.

When I get to the bedroom, I open my suitcase to get out some pajamas. I see my cell phone sitting on the dresser. I pick it up to see if I have any missed calls or text. I set it back down when I noticed Malcolm called me and I have a missed text from Hawk. I pick it up again then set it back down in a hurry. I take my pajamas into the bathroom with me to change. My heart wants to reach out to both of them. My head is telling me it's wrong. Maybe I should stop breaking Grams rules. Is it really fair to Warrick or whoever else I date in the future that I keep in contact with the guys before them?

I change my clothes and do all the nightly ritual before crawling into bed. I turn the bedside lamp off and then throw the blankets over my head. I've never been comfortable sleeping in new places.

I start tossing and turning. I've tried to shut my mind off. It's not working. This house is very quiet. It feels strange to be alone in bed. I haven't slept alone since the night in the hotel room where I met Hawk. Before that, I was in Malcolm's bed. What the hell am I doing to myself?

The harder I try to sleep the more I can't settle my mind. At this rate, I'm not getting any sleep tonight. How exhausted does a person have to be to just fall into a deep sleep? I'm physically tired. Mentally I am worn out. I should be passed out by now.

I can't take it any longer. I look at the clock for the tenth time since getting into bed. Almost two hours have ticked by. I reach over and turn the light on. I look around the room. I need something to do to help me fall asleep. As I scan the room, my eyes stop on the dresser. I get out of bed and get my phone. I run back to the bed as if I were a kid getting caught out of bed. I turn the light back off after crawling back into bed. I bring up the clock and set the alarm. All I need right now is to get up late. I put the phone down next to the pillow. Not even ten seconds later I pick it back up. I read the text message from Hawk.

Hawk: I made it back safely. It feels lonely in my bus without you. I hope you are okay! I'm here if you need me. Anytime of day!

I start typing.

Me: I'm doing alright. I miss you, too!

I use the back button and erase it. I really should

not reach out to him. I put the phone back down. Goddamn it!

Me: I miss you, too! I'm getting into bed.

I hit send. I wait for a response. Silently begging him to text back. When a few minutes pass by. I realize he's probably not going to text me back. I do another big no no in Grams rules. I call Malcolm. On the second ring, he answers.

"Hello, Ciara." I seriously miss the sound of his voice. I miss the way he says my name.

"Hey."

"How are you?"

I snuggle underneath the blankets. *"Do you remember the first night I stayed at your house?"*

"Of course. How could I ever forget having you next me!"

"I wish you were across the hall from me right now."

"I wish that, too." He pauses and I don't say anything. *"Can't sleep?"*

"I'm exhausted, but no, I can't sleep."

"I have an idea to help you. You have to close your eyes and just listen to my voice."

"Okay."

I close my eyes and listen to him talk. His voice is soothing. He is telling me all about a meeting he had today. As I have my eyes closed, I pretend he's right here with me. It's working. My eyes are getting heavier. He just keeps talking. I feel my body giving in. The last thing I hear is him telling me how much he is missing me and that he's madly in love with me. Or is this just a dream?

CHAPTER FIVE
WARRICK

This morning isn't the same as it usually is. Shay and I have an extra person at the breakfast table. A beautiful new guest. She is someone who seems to fit very well into our space. I know what you're thinking, how can I know this when it hasn't been a full twenty-four hours yet. I am a strong believer when something is right, it's right without a second thought. There's no reason to second guess this connection. Just because I think Ciara fits into mine and Shay's world doesn't necessarily mean I think we have a love connection. There is hope that we will, though. When I say she fits into our world, it means it feels like we've always known each other. We've all met someone before and say it seems like I've known you my entire life. Meeting one another has been natural. That makes me happy that I decided to meet Ciara. Love or not, she's part of our lives now. I am highly looking forward to seeing if this new found friendship can be the love I've been missing in my life. In all honesty, I am lonely. I miss human contact that is real. Yeah, I've had sexual relations with women, but nothing more than a one night stand or a weekend fling. I want everything a relationship is about. I won't lie, I am still terrified I'm not ready.

"Ciara, will you be here when I get home today?"

"I will be."

"Yay!" Shay uses her arms to show her excitement. Then she looks at me. *"Daddy, can I play with Alaska before school?"*

"You have a few minutes before the bus comes. However you need to make sure Ciara is alright with it."

"I think Alaska would love it."

Shay takes her cereal bowl to the kitchen then she goes to play with the puppy. I glance over at Ciara. She sips her coffee while watching my kid and her puppy play. I wonder if this is how every morning will go. Could this be a new routine for Shay and I? I also wonder what she thinks about being here. Is she feeling this can work as I am?

"How did you sleep?"

"Oh, umm, I slept good once I started to drift off. I almost didn't hear my alarm."

"Do you need extra blankets or anything?"

She smiles. *"No, it's perfect the way it is. Thank you, though."*

"Are you still up for going with me today?"

"Are you kidding!? I'm looking forward to going."

"Great." I get up from the table. *"Okay, little lady it's time to get you ready for the bus."*

"Ciara, are you going to watch me get on the bus?"

"I wouldn't miss it!"

We all go to the front door. I give Shay her jacket to put on, then I get her backpack off the hook. I hold it for her while she slips her tiny arms through the straps. As we walk down the driveway, Shay holds Ciara's hand instead of mine. Before I decided to place my bid to date Ciara, I thought long and hard about a bond that may form between the two of them. I wondered how Shay could handle the loss if Ciara doesn't pick us in the end. Was I going to give Shay false hope to have a mother figure in her life? I chose to do this because I know I am not going to know the outcome unless I put us on this path. If Ciara doesn't end up in our lives forever, I still need to know how it affects my daughter. As I said earlier, I am lonely. I don't want to be a single dad forever. I see this experience as a test trial for us both. The unknown is unpredictable. This could be the best thing I've done to extend our family or the worst idea I've ever had. Live and learn, right?

Shay gets on the bus. She picks a seat where she can see us. She waves goodbye with a smile I haven't seen before. My kid is happy that Ciara is here. I cross my fingers that I made the right decision. My little girl has been my everything for almost six years and I am her everything. I am the only parent she's ever had.

"Are you ready to hit the ball field?"

"Absolutely! I just need to grab my purse and phone."

We go back to the house. Ciara gets her things and I get my duffle bag. When she came back down the stairs, I noticed she put sneakers on. Smart girl. I have a few things planned for us today.

We enter the ballpark and right away Ciara's eyes light up. I kinda have those butterflies that I had as a teenage boy taking my girlfriend to a game. Baseball has been in my life since the eighth grade. When I was in high school I had my first girlfriend. The guys laughed and joked around whenever one of us got a girl and brought them into our click. To us the game came first. It's your first love if you were a true player. The girl always was a second hand love. The girls didn't care. They just wanted to date a jock and wear your letterman jacket. As we grew older and moved on some of us kept the game their first love. I was one of them. It took me years into my game to allow a woman to take over. I have no regrets. Sadly life changed without a warning for me. I went through every emotion I possibly could have. I stand here today still loving the game. Except Shay is my first love and baseball second. With any luck at all a woman will fill a void in my life. Baseball isn't going to last forever.

"What position do you play?"

"I play right field. I started playing first base but as I kept growing my coach moved me to right field. It's where I've been since my junior year in high school."

"How tall are you? I feel like a midget next to you."

I laugh. She is kinda short next to me. *"I am 6'5!"*

"No wonder I feel so short."

"So, before we go out on the field, I think I was supposed to take you shopping." I take her hand and guide her into the gift shop. *"You need some baseball gear."*

"Should I get something with Parker or Williams on the back?"

She laughs as I raise my brow. *"Neither!"* I take her over to the counter. *"Order for Winthrope,"* I tell the girl.

She goes and gets the order. Ciara can't hide her smile even though she is trying to. When she brings out the jersey, I have her give it to Ciara. She takes the paper off. Then read the shirt.

"You got me a jersey with my name on! That is so awesome!"

"You must try it on."

The girl working here takes Ciara into the dressing room area. I wait on pins and needles to see if it fits. I'll be slightly embarrassed if it doesn't. Ciara comes out from behind the curtain.

"Well, how does it look?"

"Looks perfect!"

"Thank you so much, Warrick. I love it!"

"I think you are missing something." I walk away and go over to where the baseball caps are. I pick one out and hand it to her. She giggles.

"I've never looked good in hats." She's a trooper, though and puts it on.

"Yeah, that's not the type you need." She gives back to me. I get her a different one and bend the bill of the cap. Ciara puts her hair up into a ponytail. I hand her the hat. *"Now that hat is your style."*

"Really? I don't look like a dork?"

I laugh. *"You are far from looking like a dork. I think you are pretty damn hot in my eyes!"*

"You're not so bad yourself."

"Please feel free to get anything you'd like. There's sweatshirts, tanks, pajamas, and more. I have to run up to the office to get your guest pass. I'll be right back."

I loved seeing the smile on Ciara's face. She seemed genuinely happy about the jersey. I hope I can continue to make her smile.

Today went by so fast. I took Ciara out on the field. We played catch and did some batting after she met my fellow teammates. The guys welcomed her and it was a huge relief they liked her. Ultimately it's me who has to like her, but it's nice having your teammates approval. We spend so much time together that it's nice having their support. We are just one big family. Most of them know what I've gone through. Them having my back now means the world to me.

After we spent hours out on the field a few of us went to lunch. It gave Ciara the chance to get to know my friends. I feel that's important since we are dating. I want her to know who I am. I have no intention of hiding anything. That includes the past. I know at some point I'll have to tell her about Chari, Shay's mother. I can already sense Ciara wants to ask about Chari.

We got back to my house in time to get Shay off the bus. We went into the house long enough to drop off Shay's school books. Also for Ciara to take Alaska outside for a bit. Now we are heading to Ciara's boutique. I am looking forward to stepping into her life. I want to know whatever she'll share with me. This relationship isn't just about my life. There are three of us here. Not one of us is more important than the other.

Ciara tells me that her best friend Porter works for her. She thinks the two of us will get along. She does however warn me that he is a busybody but means no harm, especially when it comes to celebrities. I am curious if he'll know who I am. If he does, I hope he doesn't know much about my past. I want to be the one who tells Ciara about me. I really don't like hearsay gossip.

We enter Ciara's boutique and she goes running into his open arms. Sorta makes me jealous. They hug and tell each other how much they miss one another. He gets a good look at her.

"Nice get-up." He looks right at me. *"Hello, I'm Porter."*

"Hello, I'm Warrick and this is my daughter Shay."

The two of them say hi to each other. *"Ciara, can I look around?"*

"Of course, Shay. Make yourself at home."

"Let me guess. Baseball clothing, you must be right fielder Warrick Winthrope?"

"That is correct. Are you a fan?"

"I watch when I can."

Ciara wraps her arm around one of mine. *"How about a little tour?"*

"I'd love that."

"I don't see any kids' clothes."

"I know. I don't have a line of children's clothes. I'm sorry."

"How come?"

"I don't have the slightest idea what kids want."

"You should ask them."

"I agree. I totally should!"

My daughter goes back to browsing. Ciara takes me into the back room where she shows me her work station. I have to admit, I know nothing about fashion. I have never been around so much fabric before. I can clearly see this is Ciara's first love. She is in her element right now. This girl keeps amazing me today.

We go back out front. Porter is being a good guy with entertaining Shay. *"So, I was thinking that we could go to Langfords Bistro for dinner."*

Porter pipes up. *"I've heard that place is amazingly good. There is a four month reservation list, though."*

"That is true. I have reservations at five for four. Porter, would you like to join us for dinner?"

Both Ciara and Porter say, *"Really?"* At the same time.

"Really! I made the reservation months ago. At the time I made them I thought maybe Ciara would want to invite Millie. You are welcome to take her place."

"Umm, I cannot go to a place that nice dressed like this."

"I happen to know a girl who makes beautiful clothing. I could hook you up," I joke.

"I hope this girl has men's clothing for you," she jokes back.

Porter is already browsing for clothes. I think this evening is going to go smoothly. I am looking forward to stepping deeper into Ciara's life.

CHAPTER SIX
CIARA

I found a dress in the back room. It's a silver glittery cocktail dress that is knee length. The back is open and has spaghetti straps. I put my hair up in a twist and used one of the hair combs Porter found in our accessory case. It is a perfect match to the dress. Porter also found a men's suit for Warrick to wear. I wasn't sure I'd have something on hand for a man of his height. I must say, Warrick looks even taller in a suit and boy, does he wear it well. I love the no tie with a vest look on him. Navy blue is definitely his color. I bet he could pull off a black suit just as well. I didn't want Shay to feel left out. I asked Warrick if I could do a few alterations to the dress she wore to school. So, I took a few measurements before I turned her plain black dress into a little cute cocktail dress. I sorta even amazed myself with what I had done in a short time frame.

We entered Langford Bistro and were taken to our table right away. As we walked through the dining room I couldn't help but notice how beautiful the place is. I also noticed Porter has a little swagger going on. I am thrilled he gets to experience this restaurant with us. I know he wouldn't get the chance to enjoy a place like this on his own. Even I know a place as this is for the rich. I could easily bring us here, I just don't tend to go out much. With the guys I've been dating lately, I see how much I deprive myself of enjoying a night out. I am learning there's more to life than being a workaholic.

I sit in between the two men in my life, Warrick and Porter. Shay is on the other side of her dad. Our table is a horseshoe booth shaped. I like that my back isn't to anyone. I like to be able to watch people. I find it entertaining.

We all pick up a menu. I lean over to Warrick. *"Have you been here before?"*

"I haven't. Jay recommended this place. He said you can't go wrong with a steak."

I met Jay today. He's cool, so I'll stick to his recommendation. When the waiter comes to take our orders, the three of us get the same thing.

Caramelized New York strip, medium-rare with a baked potato, and crispy asparagus. Shay gets chicken strips and French fries. I got a cup of New England clam chowder while the guys got salads and Shay got applesauce. Warrick ordered the best bottle of wine for us and a Shirley temple for Shay.

"So, Porter, tell me how you met this beautiful and talented lady." Warrick takes my hand under the table and laces his fingers with mine.

"Oh, gee, I believe it was ten years ago. We were at a fashion show here in New York. It was a brief conversation. Then a year later we bumped into each other again at the same fashion show. We hit it off. Ciara offered for me to come and work under her. I couldn't pass up the opportunity to learn from the best."

"Oh, stop! You were already good at what we do."

"Don't let her fool you, she taught me more than I knew."

"Sounds like it was meant to be."

Our conversation keeps going throughout dinner. Porter does his usual prying into Warrick's life. I noticed Warrick only talks about Shay or baseball. I am relieved when Porter doesn't try and snoop into his privacy. I am impressed with how Warrick stays engaged in conversation while attending to Shay as well. I find it remarkable how he can multitask. He does a kid booklet with Shay and never stops conversation with us. His social skills are right on. I have to say, Shay is a delight in public. Whatever Warrick is doing, he's doing something right.

On the car ride back to Warrick's home Shay fell asleep. He carried her up to her room and got her into bed. I went to my room. I sat on the bed and kicked my high heels off. I start checking my phone for missed calls or messages. I saw this morning that Hawk did reply to my text message last night. It must have been after I fell asleep to Malcolm's voice. I didn't have time this morning to reply because I didn't actually hear my alarm go off. I woke up later than I wanted. I hurried and took a shower so that I could join Warrick and Shay for breakfast. We left right after that. I didn't take my phone with me today because I knew I'd be tempted to text him back and that wouldn't be fair to Warrick.

I jump when Warrick knocks on the door frame like a kid getting caught doing something they shouldn't be doing. *"I was wondering if I could take you somewhere."*

"Umm, sure."

"You'll want your heels."

I pick up my heels from the floor on my way out of the room. I follow him downstairs. I wonder what he means by taking me somewhere. We can't leave the house with Shay sleeping.

"Barbara should be here any minute."

I guess we are going somewhere. *"Where are you taking me?"*

"It's a surprise."

"Thank you for dinner tonight. It was very kind of you to ask Porter to join us."

"We are in a relationship for a month and possibly longer when this is all over with. This relationship isn't just about you learning my life. It's about me learning yours as well."

"Porter loved every minute of it. He is a big part of my life. He's one of the few people that knows me very well."

"I hope to become one of those people."

I smile. *"I think you are well on your way."*

Barbara comes through the front door. Warrick thanks her for coming on short notice. He gets my coat from the hall closet and helps me into it, then we leave. I am nervously waiting to see where he is taking me. I am not used to surprises. Although, these men are beginning to change that.

Warrick drives us through the city. He's been holding my hand as he has a few times today. We talk a little bit on the way to wherever we are going. Today has been amazing. Between playing a little bit of baseball, lunch with a few of his close friends and dinner out with one of mine, I am super curious what he has up his sleeve tonight.

Warrick pulls up outside a small club that is a little bit hidden. It's nowhere near the bigger clubs that most attend. He parks the car then gets out to open my door and offers me his hand as I get out. Warrick is a gentleman. His upbringing must have been with good parenting.

We go inside and the lights are dim. The room is fuller than I anticipated. We find a small table somewhere in the middle. He asks me what I'd like to drink. When a waitress comes to our table, he orders two glasses of wine. I sit back and watch the musicians on stage. I haven't ever been into jazz music. I find myself enjoying the sound.

I lean over toward Warrick. *"They sound good."*
"The guy on the far right, he's my father."
"Oh, wow!"

"This band has been playing together for twelve years."

"That's impressive."

"I come as often as I can to see him. He's my biggest supporter and I want to return my support to him."

We listen for quite some time before Warrick asks me to dance. I am glad to be wearing high heels. God this man is so tall. I like it. I like it a lot! Not only is he tall, the man can dance. Whoever would have thought a jock would be a smooth dancer as well? I would not have never thought of it.

The song isn't over yet, but Warrick and I have stopped moving. He kisses me with yearning. I feel his emotions as his lips and tongue slow dance with mine. I hid my face when the room erupted with applause. I don't know why I feel embarrassed. The applause probably wasn't even for us. Warrick takes my hand and we leave the dance floor. He brings me down a dark hallway, then he opens a door and we slip through it. We are outside on a deck. When the door closes, my back presses against the cold metal door. I tilt my head back to see Warrick's face. His lips are on me again. This time the kiss is more avid but the emotions stay intact. I feel how much this man wants to give love and be loved in return. I feel there are layers to him that will slowly peel away. I wonder if we'll have enough time together for me to fully understand him.

"I've wanted to kiss you ever since I wiped sour cream off your top lip last night."

"A kiss like that is worth the wait."

We both start laughing when the door is pushed open and I fall into his hard chest. We move out of the way for people to come outside to smoke during the band's break. He takes a hold of my hand as we enter the building once again. I thought maybe I'd meet his father, but I don't. We exit the front entrance and get back into the car. Maybe he's not ready to peel back that layer just yet.

When we arrive back at his home for the second time this evening we go upstairs. Something is off with him. He was quiet on the drive back. I want inside his head. I want to know how he could just shut himself off after a kiss like that. Did I do something wrong?

I lean on the door frame to my room as I watch him go further down the hallway to peek in on Shay. He re-closes her door softly. When he turns around, he sees me watching him. His steps are big as he comes toward me. Except he isn't coming to me. He goes to his own bedroom door instead.

"Hey," I say quietly.

He glanced at me from over his shoulder. *"Goodnight, Ciara."*

"Did I do something wrong?"

He spins around and two steps is all it takes for him to be in front of me. *"No, you did nothing wrong. I am trying to avoid doing something wrong myself."*

"I don't understand what you mean."

"You have no idea what was running through my head before we were interrupted by those smokers."

I take his hand and pull him into my room. I don't want to be the reason Shay wakes up. *"Do you regret kissing me? If you…"*

Warrick grabs my face with both hands and kisses me. His body was pressed into mine as he backed me to the wall. *"I kissed you and I didn't want to stop."* Warrick turns away from me and walks further into my bedroom. He puts his hands inside his pant pockets. He faces away from me when he says, *"I almost didn't care that we were in a public place. If we weren't interrupted, I don't know if I would have stopped."*

I walk over to where he is and put a hand on his back. I run my hand down his spine as I move slowly around to the front of him. I step back and connect my eyes with his. I reach up for the spaghetti straps of my dress and slide them down past my shoulders as if I'm peeling back a layer of me. I see him swallow hard. My dress falls to the floor. I step out of it as I move closer to him. I reach up and unbutton a button on his dress shirt. He doesn't stop me, so I decide to undo another one. His hand goes to the back of my neck, bringing me in closer as he kisses me again. Suddenly, I'm no longer on my feet. He sets us down in a chair in my room. I straddle his lap. His lips are hot on my neck. I moan next to his ear when his palm cups my pussy. His finger then glided over my lower lips. I get up to my knees and he licks one of my nipples. I hook my thumbs into the waistband of my panties and push them to my thighs. Warrick's fingers spread me open as he entered me. I get lost in the moment of pleasure, forgetting that I was trying to remove his clothing.

I remove his hands from my body and settle back down on his lap. My panties are stretched. I undo the buttons on the vest. Then I finish unbuttoning his shirt. I open his shirt as my hands run along his chest. He helps me with removing his jacket, vest and shirt. I watch as I run my fingertips over each defined muscle off his chest and abdomen. His body is hard beneath my fingers. I undo his pants and he lifts his body to remove them fully along with his boxer briefs. I swallow when I see his girth and length. I am hesitant to go any further. I'm scared I'm going to fail. I'm not the one who usually is the aggressor. He brushes my hair over my shoulders, his hand then holds the back of my neck to bring me to his lips. I throw my head back as his teeth graze my skin. I want him inside. I need him to let me take what I want.

I get up from his lap and let my panties fall to my feet. He watches with hunger in his eyes as I cup my breasts. Then I slide a hand down my body to my pussy. I play with my clit. Warrick leans forward, grabbing my waist to bring me closer. I enter myself with my fingers. He sucks my nipple between his lips. My pussy is wet. I push his back into the chair as I straddle his lap once again. I grip onto his engorged cock and stroke him. I get to my knees and inch forward, lowering my body onto his cock. I don't take him all the way. I use his manhood for pleasure. I take more and more of him each time I come back down on his shaft.

Warrick wraps his arms around my waist, lifting me off of him. He then puts me to my feet and spins me so that my back is to his front. The next thing I know, I'm bent over the chair. My chest is pinned to the seat cushion. He enters me from behind. I gasp and moan as he thrust into me. He takes me hard.

When he pins my arms to my back, he fucks me harder and faster. I cum on his cock and that only encourages him to give me more. He leaves my hands pinned to my back as his other one grabs my throat. I orgasm again. I feel him pull himself out of me. His cock spews his orgasm on my arms and back. I lie here limp on the chair. I don't even move as I hear him get up off the floor. I want to stay here in the bliss of the orgasm.

CHAPTER SEVEN
WARRICK

Yesterday was an incredible day. I haven't felt this alive inside in such a long time. I think I did the right thing by bidding on Ciara. I should call Millie and thank her for this opportunity. With how great I feel, I just hope I can open myself up to her fully. By that, I mean I hope I can expose my past. I haven't opened that part of me to anyone. Not my family and definitely not my friends. I could never bring myself to share the pain I went through. I locked myself off and dealt with things my own way. I buried shit so far down inside, that I hid my true emotions. My family and friends tried to help me, but I wouldn't let them. I focused all my energy on being a dad. It's what I had to do or else I would have been lost.

"Daddy, are you going to get my cereal?" I look at Shay with a questioning look. *"Cereal! I have school."*

"Right!"

I get the box of cereal from the cupboard and pour some into a bowl. *"That's not the kind I eat."*

I look at the box. *"Shit!"* Shay covers her mouth with her hand and points her finger at me. *"I know. Don't repeat my naughty words."*

I get the right box out this time and use another bowl to give her breakfast. I get the milk and add some, then take it to the table where she sits.

"Is Ciara coming to breakfast?"

"I think she's still sleeping."

"Aww, I wanted her to take me to the bus."

"Eat your breakfast. Maybe she'll be down before you leave."

"Is Ciara moving in?"

"No. I told you she's only here for a while."

"You like her though."

"I do like her. You do, too, right?"

"Yes, but you really like her."

"Eat, little lady."

I pour milk into the bowl of cereal. I wasn't hungry, but I don't want to waste it. Shay has her eyes glued on me as she eats. The wheels are turning in her head. I know she wants to keep prying. I'm not ready for her to question mine and Ciara's relationship. I have to protect her from any possible heartbreak. As far as I'm concerned, Shay needs to think Ciara and I are just friends. That is why after I spent the night in Ciara's room, I made sure I was awake before Shay saw me in there.

"Okay, little lady, it's time to get you to the bus. You only have a half-day today."

"I hope Ciara will be there when I get off the bus."

I joke. *"Let's hope the sleepyhead is awake by then."* She giggles.

I took Shay to the bus then I cleaned up the breakfast dishes. I venture upstairs to check in on Ciara. I knock on her door before opening. When I peek inside she's still sleeping. I close the door then go back downstairs. We were up pretty late so I'll let her sleep longer. I go down to the basement after I get a bottle of water. I turn on my stereo for some tunes. With my favorite workout playlist playing, I warm-up and stretch my muscles before I start lifting weights. I will work my arms first, then I'll probably do chest and abs. I might squeeze in some running on the treadmill. Two more days until spring training starts. I am stoked!

I get a towel from the shelf and wipe my face. I've been in the gym in my basement for the last two hours working out. I need a shower. I shut the music off before going upstairs. When I get to the first floor, it doesn't appear as Ciara has been down here yet. I run upstairs and see her bedroom door is still closed. I'm tempted to knock but decide against it. I am hoping she is sleeping late and not avoiding me. After the incredible night together that would be disappointing to find out she's avoiding me.

I go into my room. I think about how last night unfolded. Yes, I kissed her. Yes, it was super hot. If the band didn't take a break, I'm not sure how far things would have gone. In the heat of the moment, I wanted her. I would not have cared that we would have been exposed to the public. I was ready to have sex with her right there on the back deck without a second thought. Once we were interrupted, I knew I had to get us out of there. On the drive back to the house, I thought about how easily things could have turned hot and heavy. The closer we got to my house, I decided that maybe having sex with her should wait until it was the right time and place. I was prepared to call it a night. Then she pulled me into her room. There was no denying I wanted her. It wasn't easy when I pulled back because of how much I wanted her. I only did because I want a real chance at love. I was surprised at her forwardness. Ciara doesn't seem like the girl who takes what she wants. She is more on the shy side. Once she took her dress off, there was no stopping us. The chemistry between us was bold and sizzling. We both wanted that sexual connection. Ciara is beautiful and undeniably sexy. Having her stand before me in nothing but a pair of panties I could not have turned away if I tried. Now that she hasn't come out of her room this morning, it leaves me to think maybe I should have tried harder. The sex was hot as fuck, though, so why hasn't she come out of her room today? I don't think what unfolded between us was a mistake. I don't even think it was too fast. When it's right, it's right. Maybe I'm the only one feeling it. Maybe I don't live up to the other men she's been with. Their connection could be stronger than ours.

I go and take a shower now that I have convinced

myself that I moved too fast. I have to rectify this. I am not ready for Ciara to give up on us because we acted on the sexual connection before we established a strong relationship.

When I leave the master bathroom to my room, my cell phone is ringing. I pick it up off the bedside night table. I see it is Millie calling me. I pick it up, wondering why she's calling me. My first thought is that I'm about to be yelled at or something. Maybe I am right, Ciara is avoiding me and she wants to leave. I take a deep breath before I answer the call.

"Hello!"

"Hello, Warrick. It's Millie Verbank."

"Ms. Verbank, how are you?"

"I'm doing fine, thank you. I am calling because I've been trying to reach my granddaughter. She isn't answering her phone or returning any of my calls."

I kind of feel a bit relieved. *"I believe she's still sleeping. She hasn't come out of her room today."*

"I really need to speak with her. Can you please wake her and have her return my call. As I said, it's very important."

"I will."

"Thank you. Have a great day."

I get dressed in a pair of jogging pants before I go

and knock on her door. She still doesn't answer. Now I'm just plain worried about her. I turn the knob and push her door open. She is still in bed sleeping. I go over to the side of the bed she's sleeping on and touch her cheek with my knuckles. She isn't avoiding me because of our sexual encounter last night. She is in bed because she's sick. She has a slight fever.

I leave the room and go down to the kitchen and get her a glass of orange juice. Then I get her some ibuprofen for the fever. I take it back up to her room and set it on the night table. I sit on the edge of the bed and touch her shoulder to wake her.

"Ciara, I brought you a drink and some ibuprofen for your fever." Her eyes blink open. I get the drink and the pills. *"Can you take the pills?"*

"Yeah."

She sits up slightly to have a drink and swallow down the medication. Her body slumped back into the mattress. She rolls to her side.

"Can I get you anything else?"

"No, thank you. I just need a little more sleep."

"Your Grandmother has been trying to get a hold of you. She said it's important."

"Can you please tell her I will get in touch with her later?"

"I can do that. Get some more rest."

I stand from the bed and lean over to kiss her forehead. I hope she is feeling better soon. Her puppy whines and I get her from the crate. I'm sure she needs to be taken outdoors and will want some food. After that, it should be about the time Shay will be home from her half-day of school.

CHAPTER EIGHT
CIARA

I woke this morning and the first thing I noticed was Warrick wasn't next to me anymore. I got out of bed and went into the bathroom. I took one look at myself in the mirror and went back to bed. I didn't bother seeing what time it was. I didn't care. I don't feel good. I just needed a little more sleep. I threw the blankets over my head and curled into a ball. I was shivering and just wanted to get warm again. I closed my eyes and my phone rang. I didn't bother looking to see who was calling. I did however turn the ringer off. I don't want to talk to anyone right now. I wanted to go back to sleep.

I woke again when Warrick came into the room to give me ibuprofen and orange juice. I wasn't awake for very long before I fell back to sleep. I have no idea how much time passed by between the two times

I've been awake. When I don't feel well, I sleep a lot. I am not used to anyone waking me because I have lived alone for years now. Anyone I dated in the past never bothered to ask me if I needed anything. Hunter wouldn't even call me to ask if I were any better. As if he could catch a cold over the phone. I see, now my eyes are wide open, how much of a jerk he was.

I wake once again when I feel the bed dip. I roll over and see grandma. I sit up in bed. *"Grams, what are you doing here?"*

"Warrick told me you are sick and have a fever."

"You didn't have to come for that."

"I came to bring you some stuff."

Grams sets a handbag on the bed. I open it. It has vitamin C tablets, my personal laptop, and the three-ring binder inside it. *"My laptop?"*

"You might need it going forward."

"Why, what's going on?"

"I hired a personal assistant for you."

"I don't need a personal assistant."

"You do now. Someone started gossiping about you and I don't like what they are saying. You are on a journey to find love."

"What does this gossip say?"

"They posted pictures of you with Malcolm Miller, Hawk Evans, and now with Warrick."

I grab my phone and use it to Google my name. Tears fill my eyes as I'm being called all kinds of names. Apparently, I am a slut, broke and looking for a rich man to bail out my clothing line. I am trying to dig my nails into any man that I think will benefit me. I don't have any feelings for anyone but myself. This hurts. None of it is true.

"Who would do this?"

"Someone who is shallow and jealous."

The first person who comes to mind is Bethany. She hated me. She sure did act jealous.

"I'll turn this around. I have Jacquelyn Sanders on standby."

"What is the purpose of that? My name is trash now."

"Because Jacquelyn is going to be sharing your love story from here on out. People love romance and that is what we will give them."

"You think it will work?"

"Once you are feeling better, Jacquelyn will be doing an interview with you. She'll be going back to how this all started. Starting with meeting Malcolm and your relationship with him. Same thing with Hawk. Jacquelyn will be with you right up until the wedding."

I wipe my eyes. *"So my private life is no longer*

private. What about the guys? This may cross their line of their privacy."

"I spoke with them all already."

"All ten men are fine with this?"

"Yes!"

"This is fucking crazy!"

"Sweetheart, I know it is, but can you please watch your mouth."

"This isn't fair, Grams, and you know it. This is an invasion of privacy."

"It's this or just let these tabloids destroy your reputation."

"Fuck!"

"Ciara!"

"Grams! You know I'm a private person. I don't like being in the spotlight."

"I know, sweetheart. This will be a good thing for you. Think of it as documented memories of finding love. Someday you can look back at the memories you made and see the choices you made."

"So, now Jacquelyn will be traveling with me?"

"No. We are doing everything remotely. With that said, a few pictures here and there would be nice." Grams leans forward and puts the back of her hand to my forehead. *"You need to take that vitamin C and*

some more ibuprofen. I should go so that you can rest." I hug Grams. *"Love you."*

"Love you."

This is unbelievable. I am pissed! It doesn't help that I feel like shit on top of the gossip bullshit. I grab my phone and get out of bed. I go into the bathroom and lock the door. I pace the floor then decide, fuck it, I'm calling him. I dial Hawk's number. He fucking better answer!

"Hey! How are you?"

"Have you seen the tabloids? I'm not alright!"

"I saw them. Plus your grandmother called me."

"It has to be Bethany, Hawk. That girl hates me and wants to make me look like a horrible person."

"I think this might be my fault."

"No, it's not, it's her fault."

"She is getting even with me for firing her?"

"When did you do that?"

"The minute I left you in New York. She said something about you that I didn't like, so I fired her."

Hawk and I talk for a few more minutes. I am calmer, but I'm still fired up. I need to relax. Hawk agreed with my grandmother that this new publicity with Jacquelyn will work and my reputation will be fine. I'm glad everyone thinks my love life should be this big romance show on Instagram and Twitter or whatever platform Jacquelyn is going to use.

I look at myself in the mirror and breathe out a deep breath. I tell myself I can do this. I unlock the bathroom door and go back out to the bedroom. I see the pills Grams brought to me. I need to get better before Bethany gives the tabloids any more gossip about me. Fucking bitch! I'll get even with her. Jacquelyn is going to help me do that.

I open the bedroom door so that I can go downstairs to get a drink. I walk right into a hard body. A body that I slept next to last night.

"What are you doing out of bed?"

"I was going to get a drink."

"You get back in bed and I'll get you something."

"You don't have to wait on me."

"I know I don't have to do anything." He takes my hand. *"I want to do it."*

"Okay." I'm not used to this.

Warrick feels my forehead with his lips. He then leads me into the bathroom. He sees my phone on the counter. I am glad the screen went dark. I suddenly feel guilty. I watch him as he begins to fill the bathtub. He tells me a cool bath will help my fever. I just nod my head.

"I'll have your drink ready for when you get out. What would you like?"

"Orange juice is fine."

"You got it."

Warrick leaves and I strip from the pajamas I'm wearing. I dip my foot in the water, then I get in. I turn the cold water off and leave the hot water on. It's a tad bit too cold for my liking. Once it is full enough, I play with the buttons and the jets turn on. I lie back to relax. I still can't believe I am about to expose my life to outsiders. I don't like it at all. If it weren't for Grams name being tarnished, I might have ignored the tabloids altogether.

CHAPTER NINE
WARRICK

Millie Verbank knocked on my front and I didn't know what to think. Shay was already home from school. So I asked her to take Alaska outside to play. I sat down with Millie in my living room. She explained to me all about the situation with the tabloids and how she was going to put an end to the disrespectful statements against Ciara. I have to admit having my relationship out in the open worried me. Not for myself, because I can handle criticism. What I thought about was protecting my daughter from getting caught up in bullshit that someone else started. After thinking about it, I knew I had to protect Ciara as well. I can't stand by and just let the tabloids ruin Ciara's name. She means too much to me. As far as Shay is concerned, she'll be alright. I'm taking her out of school for the next two weeks. By the time she returns, gossip that might reach her will have died down. For Ciara, this won't end for her any time soon. Especially if someone is purposely going after her. She has seven more months of this.

Millie went upstairs to see Ciara. I stayed downstairs. I wanted to give them time to talk this out. I don't see Ciara liking any of this. I figured it would be better coming from her grandmother rather than me.

While Millie went to talk with Ciara, I went outdoors to check up on Shay. I told my daughter that today was her last day of school. She was pretty excited about it. Shay really enjoys traveling with me. I also told Shay that Ciara wasn't feeling well and she said I must make Ciara some of my homemade soup. I like the idea, so I asked her if she'd like to help me. We got the pup and came back inside. I wasn't even sure if I had the ingredients. I don't know who was more thrilled that I had everything, me or Shay.

We got started right away with making the soup. I defrosted the chicken, then Shay and I measured out the water. I let her drop the bouillon cubes in. She watched it while I diced the chicken to be cooked in oil and garlic on the stove. I had the liquid on low. I laughed as Shay said it takes too long for the cubes to dissolve. I added the cooked chicken and the juices. Then I cut up carrots to add. I poured spices into Shay's hand so that she could add them. I told her we had to let it simmer before we could add the rice. By this time Millie came back down from Ciara's room. I introduced Millie and Shay to each other. It was a very brief meeting as Millie had an appointment to get to.

I went upstairs to check on Ciara. Her door opened and it caught us both off guard when she walked right into me. I basically ordered her back to bed. I can tell from her expression, it's been a very long time since someone has actually taken care of her. That ends today. I'll take care of her for as long as she is with me.

I left Ciara to bathe. I check on the soup before taking a drink up to her room. I could hear the jets in the tub running. Good, I hope she can relax while the coolness of the water helps her fever. That is when I begin to wonder what she has. I don't hear her coughing or sneezing. Why does she have a fever? I should probably ask her later. Hopefully whatever she has it is only a twenty-four hour bug. We leave the day after tomorrow. I have to be in Florida no matter what. I'd hate to make her travel while being sick. I'd also hate it if I had to go without her.

I let the soup simmer for about an hour longer. Shay wasn't excited anymore about helping. She stayed in the living room watching television with Alaska curled up on her lap. I just know my kid is going to be asking for a puppy. I will have to see if the infatuation wears off over the next few weeks. Right now the puppy is like a new toy. I cooked the chicken flavored Rice-a-Roni in the microwave as if I would if serving as a side dish. When it is done, I add it to the soup. Probably about another half an hour on simmer it will be ready to eat.

"Daddy, is Ciara coming out of her room today?"

"Probably not. Remember when you were sick a couple of months ago and you stayed in bed a few days?"

"Yes."

"That's what Ciara is doing."

"That's a bummer."

"How about you go and see if she's awake. But be quiet in case she is sleeping, we want her to rest as much as possible."

Shay goes to check on Ciara. I get a tray from the pantry. I set it all up with a bowl, spoon and a glass. It's missing something. Shay comes back to the kitchen and tells me she is sleeping. I fix us a couple bowls of soup and we eat at the breakfast table.

GRANDMA'S SILENT AUCTION

I already put Shay into bed about a half hour ago. Ciara has been in bed all day. I've been trying to leave her alone, but she needs to eat. I peeked in on her before I went to the kitchen. I left the door cracked. I warm her soup, pour her some orange juice, I take the tray up to her room. I set it on the dresser while I go over and wake her.

"Ciara, I brought you some soup." She rolls onto her back. I touch my wrist to her forehead. *"I think your fever is gone."*

"I feel a bit better. I don't really get it. I have a fever and body aches, but nothing else."

"Let's hope you get better and not worse. Shay and I made you some soup."

I get the tray and set it over her lap. *"Oh, I love chicken and rice."* She stirs it and then fills her spoon. She blows on it before trying it. *"Wow! This is really good."*

"Thanks! I made up my own recipe."

"Wait, you made this yourself?"

"I did."

"I'm impressed."

"How are you? I mean about the whole love story your grandmother is about to unfold?"

"I don't like it, but if it will not ruin the name Grams built, I'll do it."

"Why did you do this whole thing in the first place?"

"I didn't know about it. It was sprung on me. She had already auctioned me off before I found out. Why did you?"

"I haven't been in a relationship since Shay's mother. I wasn't sure if I was ready to be in one again. After Millie asked me, I thought why not at least give it a try. I do want to love again. I don't want to be alone forever."

"What happened to Shay's mother?"

"We were married a year before we had Shay. We were happy and loved each other. Chari had to have an emergency c-section. She didn't make it out of surgery."

"I am so sorry to hear that."

"I was a wreck. I hid it very well on the outside but on the inside I was broken. I didn't really grieve. I had a new born daughter to take care of. Over the years, the anger diminished. The sadness slowly faded. I heal from the outside in. I miss it. I miss having a best friend who is also your lover."

"I hope you know what a terrific father you are. You've been through hell. It takes guts to try again. I

don't know if I could take a chance knowing I might not get picked."

"It's really no different than meeting someone in a bar or on the street. There's no guarantee when you meet someone how long a relationship will last."

"That's true! I'm glad you picked me."

"I am too."

Ciara finished all of her soup. I was getting ready to leave her alone for the rest of the night, but she asked me to stay longer. I laid back on the bed and she snuggled up next to me. We talked some more then we put a movie on. I really like having her in my arms.

CHAPTER TEN
CIARA

The last couple of days have been pretty hectic. I sure am glad whatever bug I had was only a twenty-four-hour thing. We only had one day left at his home before we had to pack and get ready to catch a flight to Florida. Warrick's spring training starts today. Yesterday, I got to meet Martha Lindblom. She is the person who watches Shay while Warrick is working. She also is the one who homeschools Shay. Martha is a very nice lady. She has been with them since Shay was born, like Barbara. I would say Warrick took his time in figuring things out between his career and being a single father. I think he's a very strong-willed man to have come up with the best care for his daughter and his career on top of mourning the loss of his wife. My heart felt for him when he opened up to me about his late wife, Chari. I heard the pain that still remains inside of him in his voice. I don't know if I could bear a loss as such. I would crumble. I don't believe I could handle it the way he did if I were in his shoes. I did learn something from him opening up to me. I learned that if I were to end up with him, he would love with all of his heart. He'd protect me as much as he protects Shay. If he loved me, I don't think I'd ever have to question it. Once he loves someone, he does it with heart and soul.

We settled into our hotel room last night. Warrick, Shay and I are sharing a room. Martha has an adjoining room. I have to admit, it was weird sleeping in a room with Warrick and Shay in the bed next to mine. The last few nights Warrick has slept beside me. He always slipped out of bed before Shay woke up. I see how much more difficult this will be now with us all sharing one room. I wonder how this will affect our growing relationship. I understand him wanting to portray this as us just being "friends" in his daughter's eyes. On the other hand, I feel it could damage our relationship later on. There is a fine line that he is trying to not cross and I see that. I guess going further, we will have to become creative if we want to be more than friends at the end of this.

Warrick is over in Martha's room getting Shay ready to start her studies. We will be leaving shortly to go to the ball field. I am excited to see Warrick in his element today. I'll get to see him play and see my first baseball game. Well, sort of. Technically this game doesn't count for stats or anything. It is probably the closest I will get to an actual game. Unless I end up with Warrick at the end of all this. Then baseball will become part of my life.

"Are you ready to get out of here?"

"I sure am." I jump up from the bed and smile. *"I am so looking forward to this."*

Warrick smiles. *"Look at you all cute and shit in baseball clothing with my name on it."*

Warrick gets his duffle bag then we leave the hotel room. He holds my hand as we take the hallway to the elevators. When we get outside, we don't get on the bus as most of his teammates do. We get in a black SUV. I give Warrick a questioning look. He told me he has a surprise later so we needed to drive ourselves. I feel giddy inside. I am also thankful for some alone time with him. We haven't had much of that in the last couple of days.

"Tell me something about yourself that I don't know yet."

"I am adopted. My biological parents are Brazilian."

"I would have never thought that. The man I saw on stage, you resemble him."

"He's my biological father. He doesn't know I am his son."

That really shocks me. I would have never thought this about him. We have something in common, sort of. *"Have you ever spoken to him?"*

"I have a few times. He is a nice man. The thing is, he doesn't even know about me. I met my biological mother about seven years ago. She told me how I could find him. She never told him about me because she knew she wasn't going to keep me. She felt it was the right thing to do. I haven't ever figured out how to tell him or even if I should tell him. I just like to go and listen to him play because he supports me. The first night we met, I found out he watches me play ball and that I am his favorite player."

"My mother left me. My grandmother raised me. I have no idea who my father is. If I ever found out, I'm not sure I could disrupt his life. Sometimes I think leaving the unknown alone is best."

"Do you have contact with your mother?"

"Nope, none. It doesn't bother me either. I feel she lost the right to know me."

"I knew from a young age I was adopted. I never let it define who I am. I have great parents."

"Grams gave me everything I needed. She loved me enough for ten people."

We arrive at the ball field and when we are walking in, fans wait outside the entrance, hoping to snag an autograph from their favorite players. This makes me uneasy with the gossip bullshit happening about me. I haven't talked with Jacquelyn yet. We have a meeting set up for tomorrow. I stay close to Warrick. He makes me feel a bit safer. But, also by doing this, I am giving whoever a chance to take pictures of me and Warrick being seen as a couple. Frankly, it's no one's business what I do with my life. I am not hurting anyone by trying to find love. Sometimes having a name that people know is not for the better.

The game just ended and it was so thrilling to watch Warrick play baseball. I left the stands when the game ended and made my way to where he instructed me to meet him. He came out from the locker room with a huge smile on his face. He took my hand and we started to walk away. His teammates hooting in the background.

"Well, what did you think?"

"I thought it was so fucking cool. That homerun you hit was the best part."

"Hey, I thought that catch was pretty awesome. That should have been at least a two-base hit."

"Oh, it was. Thank you for bringing me. I had so much fun."

"Did you get anything to eat?"

"Nah, I was glued to my seat."

"You cannot come to a game and not have a dog."

"A hotdog? I don't eat hot dogs."

"What? You have no idea what you are missing. I have to get you one."

He is nuts if he thinks I am eating a hot dog. Those are gross! I mean, I think they are, I don't really know as I have never eaten one. It's not like I couldn't have tried one before, I just never found them to be appealing. I would rather stick to a cheeseburger.

Warrick takes me to the concession stand and he orders two dogs as he calls them. He also orders a corn dog. We decide to eat while watching the next ball game that is taking place. We sit in the stands and he puts the hot dog to my lips. I shake my head no.

"C'mon you have to try it at least once."

"I'll try the one on the stick."

He laughs at me. He dips the corn dog into the ketchup before holding it to my mouth. I take a tiny bite. I shake my head no. *"Eww,"* I say after swallowing.

He takes a big bite and moans. *"It's like heaven on a stick. Try a hot dog on a bun."*

'Do I have to?"

"You don't, but it will make the whole baseball experience full."

"Fine." I take a bite of the hot dog that has ketchup and mustard on it. It's not bad, but nothing I'd want to eat every day.

We finish eating the hot dogs then we leave. I have no idea where Warrick is taking me, but I am excited to find out. Warrick is different today. He is exhilarated. It is as if baseball fills something deep down inside him that it makes him come alive. I see this same reaction whenever Shay comes home from school or in the mornings when he first sees her. Baseball and Shay truly are his loves.

"You are taking me to a private resort?"

"Yep. thought we would check out the pool."

"I don't have a bathing suit. We have a pool at the hotel."

"Not like this one." He winks at me. What does he have up his sleeve?

CHAPTER ELEVEN
WARRICK

I got a kick out of watching Ciara try a hot dog. It was as if I was telling my daughter to eat her vegetables. Hot dogs aren't for everyone. I have to admit they are much better in New York. I am happy she at least tried to eat a full one. We stuck around the ball field long enough to catch a little bit of the next game and eat. I didn't much care to stay and finish the game because I have something special planned for us. I realize, having my daughter with us, alone time is going to be hard to come by. If we are going to build something memorable, I have to be creative. I did my research and I think I found the perfect place to take her.

When we arrive at the resort that I found in my research, her expression was priceless. I checked us in and was given a key. Again her expression was funny. She hasn't figured out what we are doing. I told her we are going to the pool and it was cute to see her confusion as we have a pool at our hotel. What she doesn't know is there is privacy here that we won't find elsewhere.

I stop outside the door of a tiny building. *"What's going on?"* she asked as her eyes scanned the area.

I got the door open and pulled her inside. *"What's going is this."* I kiss her and damn does it feel good to have her lips on mine again. *"We don't have to be just friends here."*

She smiles really big. *"I like the sound of that."*

I pick her up off her feet and carry her over to the sofa in the room. *"It's no bedroom, but it's private."*

"Works for me."

When we get situated on the sofa, she sees the display of wine, grapes, cheese, and crackers. Ciara scoots closer to me. I pop the cork on the wine and pour us each a glass. *"To our growing relationship."*

We clink our glasses. I watch her take a sip. She nods her head with approval. I look into her eyes as I brush her hair from her cheek, tucking it behind her ear. How have I become lucky enough to be here with her? I never wished I had met someone sooner until meeting her. I sure as hell wish I was her one and only. I try not to think about the fact that in a few short weeks, I have to let her go. I barely know her and I already don't want her to be with anyone other than me.

"You are such a beautiful lady."

Her hand comes to my cheek. She leans in and kisses me. I take her glass and sit it on the table. She scoots closer to me and her hands interlocked behind my neck. Our bodies move together as she lies back on the sofa. I lift her legs and then cover her body with mine. I want this woman. I want to feel her skin on mine. I want to be the one that gives her the sexual pleasure she desires. Mostly, I want to be the man she wants to be with. The one she wakes up next to every day. I want to hear her laugh and be the reason she smiles. I haven't felt this way in a very long time. I don't want these emotions to ever diminish. I will be heartbroken if she doesn't pick me.

I kiss Ciara's neck. Her hands move into my hair. I want to take this moment slowly, but I also want to rip her clothes off. I want to feel the warmth of her skin against mine right this second. I slip a hand up under her shirt. Her skin is so smooth underneath my hands. I cup her breast. She moans. Her hands grabbed the back of my shirt and she lifted. I finished removing my shirt for her. She removes hers and I watch as she takes her bra off. Her breasts are full and perfect. The nipples are erect and pink in color. My cock throbs to be inside her. I pull her pants down her legs. My mouth waters. I stand and remove my pants. My shaft is fully hard and ready. Ciara gets up to her knees and she runs her hands down my chest. When she reaches my cock, her hand wraps around the girth. I grab her neck and bend to kiss her. I groan in her mouth as she strokes my manhood.

The kiss is broken, she looks me right in the eyes. She changes her position on the sofa and she sucks my cock between her lips. I close my eyes as I throw my head back. Her mouth on me feels incredible. I lift my head and watch her taking my cock in her mouth. I tell myself to let her please me. What I really want to do is grab her head and have my way with her mouth. I groan again when she takes my shaft deeper. She cups my balls and fuck, I am going to cum. I try to pull out, but she doesn't allow it. Her lips tighten, she sucks harder and I can't hold the orgasm back. I cum down her throat. She licks her lips and I take her chin and kiss her aggressively. I'm letting her know it's my turn to be in control.

I wrap my arms around her thighs and lift her. I put her on her ass, and pull her to the edge of the sofa cushion. I bend forward to lick her lower lips and dart my tongue inside of her. The taste of her on my taste buds just makes me want her more. I suck on her clit and her nails dig into my scalp. I reach up and pinch a nipple. Her moans fill the room. My cock is at full attention wanting to be where my tongue is. I'm not stopping until I have her orgasm in my mouth.

Ciara's body is trembling. I wrap my arms around her thighs to hold her in place. I lick and fuck her pussy with my tongue. She says my name and tells me she's going to cum. I use my fingers to play with her clit. I want it. I want her to let it all go.

I get up to my knees after her orgasm and kiss her. I thrust my hips and my cock penetrates her. Her nails scrape the skin on my back. Her tight pussy grips my cock tighter with each thrust. I love the feeling of being inside her. I love taking her body as mine and claiming her orgasms. This is more than sex. This is expressing our feelings for one another and connecting on a level that most couples don't ever experience. This is love and sex all in one passionate emotion.

Ciara sits up and her mouth is on mine. I thrust my hips and she moves closer to the edge of the cushion, allowing me in deeper. Her mouth moves from mine and travels to my ear.

"I am going to cum. I want you to cum inside of me, Warrick."

Her breath is hot on my neck as her moans fill my ear. Her body tenses. Then all at once, she goes limp. I thrust into her a few more times before I give her my orgasm.

CHAPTER TWELVE
CIARA

Warrick and I have been sneaking away for the last two and half weeks to the resort he found. Not every day, but close to every other day. It's really the only time we have together that we can be intimate. I think we have done a good job of keeping our hands to ourselves when we are with his daughter. If I am being truthful, it's not as easy as it sounds. Sometimes I wonder if we should be hiding our relationship from Shay. I think she knows we are more than friends. She has made comments quite a few times that we like each other. A few times it's as if she's teasing us. The girl may only be almost six, but kids see things even when we are trying to hide certain things from them.

Warrick and I are laying together on the sofa. There are no clothes between us. He is flat on his back and I am draped over him. His fingertips are rubbing my back. My head is laying on his chest. His heart beats beneath my ear. We aren't talking. We are just enjoying being in each other's arms. I like where I am at. It's never too far from my thoughts that I liked being in Malcolm or Hawk's arms as well. I know I'm in deep trouble. There's got to be someone in the next seven months that I don't fall for, right? I cannot get to the end of this and love ten men. That can't be possible. There has to be some that I don't give my heart to. It's pretty sad that I hope I don't like the next and the guy after that one. I've been with three guys and those three men I could see myself with them all. They all have qualities that fit the person I want to be with. Love and have a family.

"What are you thinking about?"

"That I'm leaving you tomorrow."

"I'm thinking about that as well."

I lift my head and move my arm to cross over his chest. I rest my chin on my forearm. I look Warrick in his beautiful Brazilian eyes. *"Could you see yourself being with me?"*

"Without a doubt in my mind." He tucks my hair behind my ear. *"Are you questioning my feelings for you?"*

"More like I am questioning myself."

"What are you asking yourself?"

"What if I don't know what true love is? I don't even really know how you feel about me."

"I wake up every morning wanting to see your face. I can't wait to hear you laughing or singing in the shower. I love seeing your eyes light up when I leave the ball field and find you. I hate having to slip out of bed before Shay wakes up. I am crazy in love with you, Ciara."

"I want to be honest with you. I don't want to hurt your feelings though."

"If you don't love me, it will hurt but I kinda need to know. I am ready to put my life on hold for you."

"It's not that."

"Tell me what it is. If you love me we can work through it together."

I get up and sit on the floor. I bring my knees to my chest. I lean my forehead on my arm. I can't stop the tears from falling. I'm so goddamn confused. Warrick sits up on the sofa and his legs are on each side of my body. His arms wrap around me from behind.

"I'm sorry for crying like a baby."

"You never have to hide your emotions from me. Tell me what is going on in your head."

"I have all these feelings inside. They are all

mixed up, though. I fell in love with you. I can't lie to you or hide the truth from you. I fell in love with the other two guys before you as well. How am I supposed to know what is real and what is living in the moment?"

I get up off the floor and walk away from this sweet man. I can't even look at him right now. I cannot bear to see hurt in his eyes. He opened his heart to me and I feel like I just stomped on it. With everything he's already endured, I don't want to be the one who crushes him. I don't want to hurt him. I want to face him and be in his embrace forever. I can't do that because I don't know if he's my forever person. Last month I wanted Hawk to be the one I love. Two months ago, I cried for days after leaving Malcolm because I loved him. I don't want to do this anymore. I don't want to go through another breakup just to see who I love the most in the end.

I start gathering my clothes from the floor. Warrick comes up behind me and puts his arms around me. *"I wouldn't want to be in your shoes. You want to know what true love is? It's when you can be faced with life's toughest challenges and when the challenge is over, you look around and see who stood beside you. You will see who is the one who holds your heart when the smoke clears."* He kisses the back of my head. *"I want to be the one who holds your heart. But if I'm not, you gave me something I was missing and that's hope. I now know I can love again and I owe that to you. My feelings for you won't change regardless if I'm the man for you or not. I'll always be here for you even if it's just for friendship."*

"Right this minute I want the friendship and the love you have to offer. I want to say, the hell with everyone else in this world and just let it be the two us. The three of us, you, me, and Shay."

He turns me so that I must face him. *"I wish it were that simple. I would love to tell you to stay. I hate this, but I have to tell you that you have to go through the challenge. I swear, Ciara, I will be here waiting for you to pick me."*

I hug Warrick tight to my body. I don't want to let him go. He's right, though, I have to go through this challenge to figure out what I want. I can only pray I figure out who I want. I'm so damn scared I'll feel all this love and I end up alone. I can't bear the thought of going through all these mixed up emotions and confusion just to end where I started from, alone.

"I want to take you somewhere. I have one more night with you and I want to make it a night you won't forget."

"Can we stay here in our little love shack a little longer?"

He lifts my head and kisses me. Then I am lifted off my feet. I wrap my legs around his waist. His skin, his scent, and his warmth is all I want right now. Selfishly, I want to feel his love for me. I need it right now. I feel I am about to break emotionally.

Warrick puts me back to the floor. *"As much as I'd like to stay here longer, we can't. Trust me you will like what I want to show you."*

He bent down and picked up my clothes and handed them to me. I don't start getting dressed until he does. I guess our little place for our lovemaking is over. I can't help but to feel sad about it. I needed him and he can't give that to me. This just proves our time together is ending.

CHAPTER THIRTEEN
WARRICK

It wasn't easy telling Ciara to put her clothes on. Trust me when I say I'd love to keep her here forever with me. I have fallen for the girl hard. I didn't think it would be possible to have strong feelings for another woman other than my first wife. She proved to me that love can happen more than once. I feel blessed that she is the woman I opened my heart to.

Ciara not only accepted me into her life, but she accepted Shay as well. She never expressed she couldn't be in the relationship because I had a daughter. I thought it could have made this a no-deal for Ciara. It relieved me on day one walking into my kitchen and seeing how well Ciara had acceptance toward Shay. I found the perfect person to add to my family. I need to show her what that will look like. There's only one way to do that.

"Are you ready?"

"As ready as I'll ever be." I hear disappointment in her voice.

I give her my best smile. *"Trust me, I'll make it up to you tonight. Your body will be mine to do as I please then I'm going to hold you in my arms all night."* That puts a smile on her face.

I have a car waiting for us when we check out of the resort. The driver already knows where we are going. Ciara watches out the window. She tells me that she's going to miss the warmth of the Florida sun. I take her hand that I'm holding and bring it to my lips. I know what she's doing. She's making small talk to avoid talking about us. I let her continue doing that. I sort of don't want her to be paying attention to where we are going. If she noticed she didn't say anything about not heading to the hotel we've been staying at. We definitely are not going back there.

We take the twenty-minute drive. Ciara twists her body to look out the window. She is surprised by being at the airport. *"I'm going back home right now?"*

"We are going home."

"You are coming with me? You have a game this evening."

"I might have pulled some strings."

"What about tomorrow's game?"

"I got everything covered."

"Wow!"

"Shay is so happy to be seeing you tonight."

"Aww, babe, I can't believe you set this up. I thought I would be going home alone. It was really stressing me out." She throws herself into my chest. I put my around her.

"We better go or we will miss our flight."

"Wait, I didn't get my dog or my stuff." I point to the front seat where Alaska is. Her luggage is in the back. *"Oh."* She giggles.

"Let's go, girl. We have a plane to catch."

We walked into my house hours later. Shay, who has been home for the last week with Barbara comes running into my arms. I am hugging her to my chest when she kisses my cheek.

"Ciara!" She screams with excitement. Ciara opens her arms and I pass my daughter to her. I put my arm over Ciara's shoulder. I clear my throat to get

her attention. *"Ciara, I'd like you to meet my parents, George and Cathy. Mom, dad this is Ciara."*

Ciara's eyes get big. I sure did surprise her. They shake hands and then we move into the living room. My mother starts asking Ciara questions about her family, what she does for a living, and so on. Ciara is being a trooper and appeasing my mother. My parents seem to really like Ciara. I think my father is impressed. I don't need my parent's approval, but it helps to have it. I could have waited to see if I am the guy she picks, however, I wanted Ciara to fully see into my life. The life I want her to be a part of forever.

My parents stuck around for a few hours then they left. I ordered the three of us dinner. I got us food from the same Mexican restaurant as before. To make this night even better and more memorable, we had another carpet picnic. The three of us ate in the living room and enjoyed another Disney movie. I have my girl on one side of me and my daughter on the other. I love every second of it. I want this life. I want us to be a family. I would get down on one knee right this second and ask Ciara to marry me if I could. I know what I signed up for. I have to see this through. I can only hope from here on out that she picks us in the end.

The movie ends and I tell Shay it's time to say goodbye to Ciara. I explain to my daughter that Ciara has things she needs to attend to. Shay asks if Ciara will be coming back for her birthday next week. Ciara teared up and said she would try. We both know that's not going to happen. My girl will be with another man.

"It's time for bed, little lady."

Shay gives Ciara a big hug. *"I love you."*

"I love you, too."

"Hello!" A voice says behind us.

All three of us look. Martha is here to watch Shay for me. Barbara's son is in town and I didn't want to pull her away from that. *"Martha is going to get you into bed. I have to take Ciara someplace."*

"Okay, Daddy."

They leave the room and Ciara questions me. *"Where are we going?"*

"You'll find out."

"You are full of surprises today, Mr. Winthrope." I wink at her and smile.

"Once we get Alaska, we can go."

I get Ciara's suitcase by the door and she carries her puppy out to my car. I drive us through the city. I think Ciara is upset with me. She has been quiet on the drive. I park outside Ciara's apartment. She looks at me. Her eyes hold sadness. I understand that as I have the same look in mine. I cannot believe this is our last night together. This month went by too fast.

"What's going on?"

"I'm bringing you home. You have spent the last month living inside my world. I want to spend the night with you inside your world."

"Are you staying the night at my apartment with me?"

"I am if you'll let me." She reaches across the counsel and hugs me. I laugh. *"I will take that as a yes!"*

"You make me so happy."

We go into Ciara's apartment and she gives me a tour. It is a much smaller place than mine, but it's a cute place. She shows me the bedroom last. I sit at the foot of her bed. I use my finger to tell her to come to me. She stands between my legs. I put my hands to her waist. Then take the hem of her shirt and lift it.

"I think I promised you that your body is mine to do whatever I please to it."

I unbutton her blue jeans then push them past her hips. She bites her bottom lip. I strip Ciara of all her clothing. I kiss her chest between her breasts. My fingers spread her pussy open as I entered her body. I find the spot that makes her moan. I press my thumb against her clit. I play with her body until my fingers are wet. I rub her juices over her nipples and suck it off each one. I am going to give Ciara multiple orgasms tonight. Starting with my tongue then she is going to cum on my cock. When she thinks she can't orgasm again, I'm going to keep taking my sweet time with her body until she has another mind-blowing orgasm. This night will not be easily forgotten. I plan on making love to her for the rest of the night, then she will fall asleep in my arms.

CHAPTER FOURTEEN
CIARA

I roll over and pull the blanket up to my chin. I reach over to the other side of the bed and it's cold. It must be that time of morning Warrick had slipped out of bed so that Shay doesn't catch him in here. I am half falling back to sleep when I remember, I'm not in his guest bedroom. I am in my own apartment. This is my bed. Warrick is gone.

I roll over onto my stomach and bury my face in the pillow. The tears had already started when I realized this isn't the guest's room in Warrick home. Another relationship equals another break-up. I even know it's going to happen and I still am not prepared for it. Breakups suck!

I throw the blanket back. I am not doing this any longer. I wipe the tears from my eyes. I bring the pillow Warrick slept on to my nose and smell it. We are not breaking up. We are on pause. That's all there is to it. He doesn't get to just slip out of bed without a goodbye. I am not going to allow that to happen.

I gather some clothes from my closet and take them to the bathroom with me. I turn the shower on and it feels kind of weird to be in my apartment. I get in and wash, then condition my hair. I think about how I am going to knock on his door and give him a piece of my mind. I am upset that he didn't let me say goodbye. There are things I wanted him to know. Things I needed him to know. It was important to me.

I get out of the shower and wrap my hair up in a towel. I open a drawer on the vanity to get some makeup out and start applying it. I think about knocking on his door and I hope he'll be happy to see me. I can surprise people too.

An hour and forty-five minutes later, I pull into Warrick's driveway. I don't see his car, but maybe he has it in the garage. I check myself in the rearview mirror. I use my hands to fluff my hair. I am a bit nervous. I tell myself there is no reason for it. I know Warrick, he knows me. This will be a good thing. I get out of my car and walk to his front door. When I reach the door, I try the handle. It doesn't open. I ring the doorbell. Nothing happens. I ring it again. I come to realize nobody is here. I turn around and walk back to my car. Just like that, he's out of my life. Seven more months until I get to see him again.

On my drive back to my apartment, I think about all the ways I can avoid falling in love with another man. I am going to break all of Grams rules. The best thing about that, nobody can stop me. It's time I take control of the outcome of my life. I will show these men I am not weak. They just can't become part of my life and then pass me onto the next guy. Love doesn't work that way.

I run up the stairs to my apartment and grab my bag that has the three-ring binder in it. I flip open to April's page. Kaiden Marcellus is about to see me breaking rule number one. Watch out Kaiden I am about to come a few days early to Nevada. Your plan to meet me at the airport is about to be broken.

I take my suitcase into my room and dump out the dirty clothes. I get clothes from my closet and put them inside. I zip it and bring it out by the front door. I smile. It feels good to be in control. I go to my laptop and book a plane ticket. I leave in two hours. I am feeling pleased with myself. Kaiden is not going to be prepared for me. I am not just talking about showing up early. He isn't going to know what hit him when I make him hate me instead of loving me.

I go to the refrigerator to get a bottle of water.

That's when I see it. I take the note off the refrigerator door to read it. I lean against the cupboards and slide to the floor.

Dear Ciara,

This past month has been absolutely amazing. I fell so deeply in love with you. You are such an amazing woman and I see myself asking you to marry me someday. When I think about the future, I cannot see it without you in it. You not only make me happy, but you do my daughter as well. Getting to know you has been a pure blessing. If you pick me to love forever, I'll be here waiting with open arms. I love you.

I know you are probably upset with me for slipping out early this morning. It wasn't easy to do that. You were peacefully sleeping and I wanted to wake you. I seriously did. I thought about how this goodbye would be easier for us both if I didn't. The next seven months are going to be tough. The unknown is sometimes scarier than we think. I just want you to know not a day will go by that I don't think about you. As much as I don't want to leave you, I have to get back to spring training. Shay and I will probably be gone by the time you read this. You know how to reach me if you need anything at all. A shoulder to lean on, a friend who understands you and loves you. - Warrick

I didn't want to cry again. I am supposed to be taking control of me. Then my sweet man breaks me again. I feel the loss of him wash over me once again. I cry and cry some more. I don't want to feel this sadness and hurt anymore.

I get off the floor. I need to get out of my apartment. Having Warrick here last night, I can smell his cologne lingering in the air. I need to get away from it for my own sanity. I grab my keys and luggage. Here I come Nevada, I hope you are ready to not meet the love of your life Kaiden Marcellus.

ABOUT THE AUTHOR

Thank you so much for taking the time to read Grandma's Silent Auction March. Word-of-mouth is crucial for any author to succeed. If you enjoyed the book, please leave a review on Amazon. Even if it's just a sentence or two. It would make all the difference and would be very much appreciated. – OXOX Michael James

Website: http://michaeljames-author332.bravesites.com/

ALSO BY MICHAEL JAMES

If you enjoyed Grandma's Silent Auction March, you may also like my other books:

The Way We Love series:

Pink Skies At Night

Shadows At Night

Nights Are Unlimited

Concealed By The Night

Shattered At Night

Freed At Night

Winning A Cowgirl's Heart - Trilogy:

The Rodeo King

The Best Friend

The Fate Of My Heart

Winning a Cowgirl's Heart -Complete Box Set

Construction Vs. Corporate- Trilogy:

Unbalanced

Balancing

Balanced

Secrets Within a Club

Club Comrade

Revenge

Saving Club Conrad

Masquerade Saga

His Pearls

His Secrets

His Prison

His Games

His Moves

All His

Crime in Landkaster series

The Mirror

Times Like These

Lonely Road of Faith

Grandma's Silent Auction series

January

February

Standalone:

Toying With October

Pieces Of Me

A Christmas For Eve

Dom Diaries: Tangled Up In You

Christmas Scavenger Hunt

Blue Christmas

Stealing the Christmas Spotlight

Co-written with Jodi Fahey

Last Sheet

Manufactured by Amazon.ca
Bolton, ON

44035023R00063